Mr. Bat
WANTS a Hat

To mischief and sparkles,
and all the brightness you bring.
~ K B

To Massimo ~ L W

American edition published in 2022
by New Frontier Publishing Europe Ltd
www.newfrontierpublishing.us

First published in Great Britain 2021
by New Frontier Publishing Europe Ltd,
Vicarage House, 58-60 Kensington Church Street, London W8 4DB
www.newfrontierpublishing.co.uk

Distributed in the United States and Canada by Lerner Publishing Group Inc.
241 First Avenue North, Minneapolis, MN 55401 USA
www.lernerbooks.com

Library of Congress Cataloging-in-Publication data is available.

ISBN: 978-1-913639-98-3

Designed by Verity Clark • Printed in China

10 9 8 7 6 5 4 3 2 1

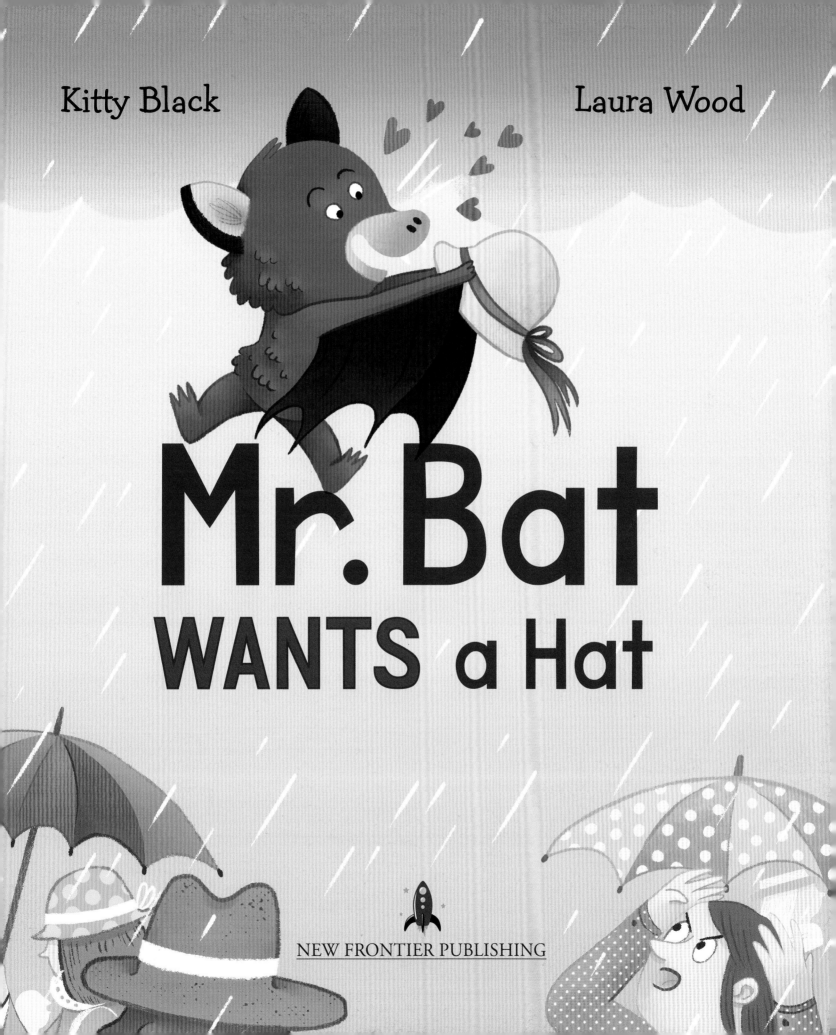

Kitty Black

Laura Wood

Mr. Bat
WANTS a Hat

NEW FRONTIER PUBLISHING

Mr. Bat was a **happy** bat.

He spent his days doing his favorite things:

and **meeting** interesting **insects**

(but not for long).

Yes, he was content . . .

until one twinkling twilight when he flew above the park.

"What is this?" cried Mr. Bat. His eyes boggled and his heart **boomed**.

"Hats!" he whispered.

"I never knew what was missing from my life!" cried Mr. Bat.

He bunched up his
batty legs and . . .

"Out of my way!" cried Mr. Bat.

"How dare you attack an almost endangered species!"

A bat!

"It's MISTER Bat actually," said Mr. Bat, "and I'm **not** leaving!"

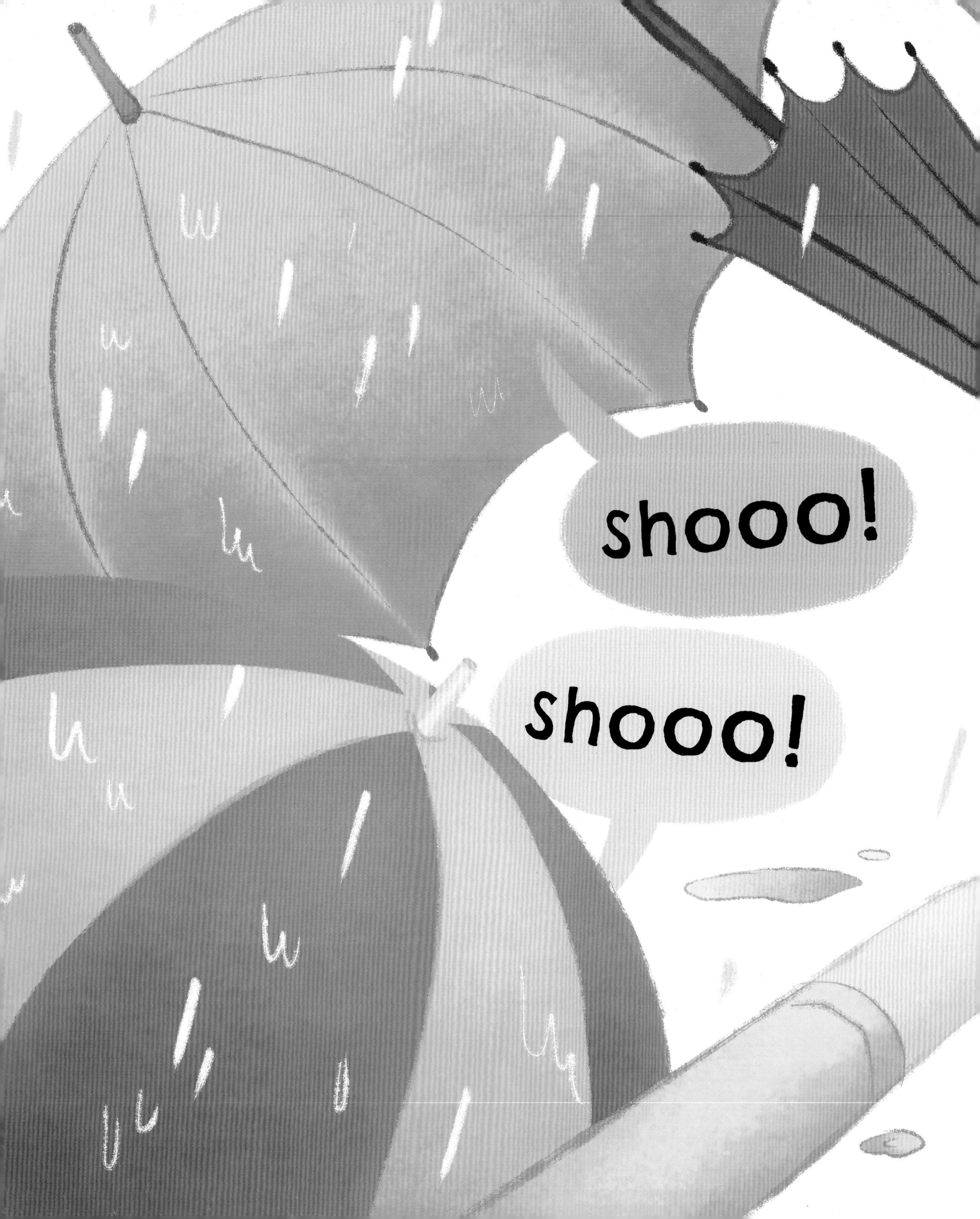
shooo!
shooo!

Okay, now I'm leaving!

Mr. Bat was not having a nice time.
"All I want is my own hat!" he sobbed.

Something caught his eye.
It had a yellow band.

With pink roses.

And shining beads.
And all covered in . . .

(Mr. Bat could
hardly stand it.)

. . .GLITTER!

He checked for umbrellas.

His eyes narrowed.

His wings arched.

His feet tucked.

SWOOP!

Success!

Oh happy day!

Oh joyous occasion!

"Oh. A sad baby. She likes hats too," said a small part of Mr. Bat.

"Too bad!" said the rest of him, dancing in his brand-new hat.

Nyeh!

He poked out his batty tongue and swung his batty bottom.

The baby cried.

"And the Best Dressed Bat Award goes to . . .

Mr. Bat!"

said Mr. Bat.

"Oh thank you!" Mr. Bat bowed to his adoring audience, "What an honour it is . . . for YOU, to admire me and my lovely hat!"

wahhhh!

The baby cried.
Louder.

"Everyone **sing!**" cried Mr. Bat.
"For he's a jolly good baa-at,
for he's a jolly good baa-at!"

wahhhh!

Mr. Bat sighed.

He stepped out of the conga line and canceled the party.

One final,
gentle
swoop.

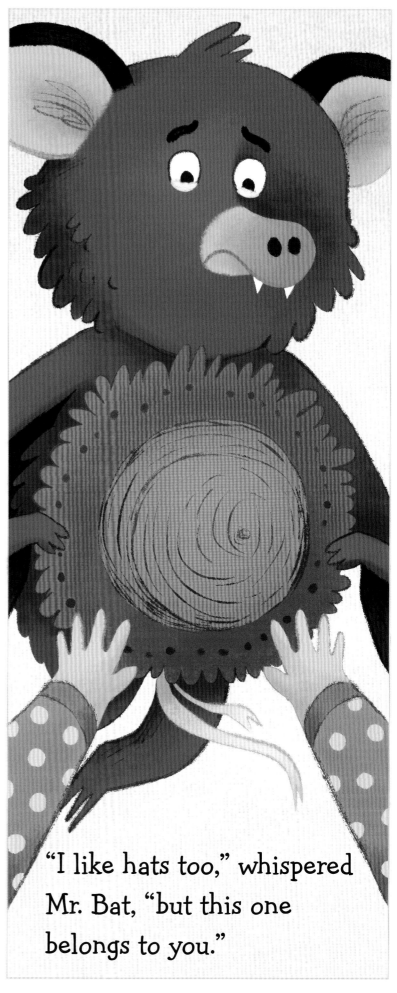

"I like hats too," whispered
Mr. Bat, "but this one
belongs to you."

A gift.

"For *me*?" asked Mr. Bat.

"Oh, I couldn't!"

But he did.

"Hats are *so* last season anyway," said Mr. Bat.

And off flew the Winner of the Best Dressed Bat Award, with a song floating on the breeze:

"For he's **a jolly good** baa-at . . ."